KT-545-008

First published in 1987 by
André Deutsch Limited
105–106 Great Russell Street, London WC1B 3LJ

ISBN 0 233 98090 3

Printed in Great Britain by Cambus Litho, East Kilbride

JANINE AND THE CARNIVAL

Iolette Thomas

Illustrated by
Jennifer Northway

ANDRE DEUTSCH

"Mummy," said Janine, "may I telephone Granny?"

"Do you know Granny's telephone number?" asked her mother.

"Yes," replied Janine, "I know our number, too, and our address."

"Okay then," laughed her mother, "but just this once, mind. And don't talk for too long!"

"I won't," promised Janine. She dialled the number carefully, and, when her grandmother answered, said, "Hello, Granny, it's me,

Janine. Are you going to the Carnival this afternoon?"

"Yes," said her grandmother.

"So am I," said Janine.

"Good," said her grandmother, "maybe we'll see each other there. I'll wear my blue jacket, so use your sharp eyes to keep a good look out for me."

But when the time came to leave, baby was hot and kept on crying.
"She's teething," said mother. "I think we'd better stay at home."
"No!" wailed Janine. "You *promised* we could go to the Carnival."
"I'm really sorry," said her mother, "but I didn't know baby would be sick when I promised."
"It's not fair." Janine looked at her father. "I've never been to a Carnival," she pleaded.

Her father winked. “Perhaps we can talk Mummy round,” he said, and suddenly Janine was sure her father would take her after all.

It was a lovely, sunny afternoon and they met lots of other people, all going to the Carnival. Janine had on her new shorts and best t-shirt; she had a red band with bobbing gold hearts in her hair and she had a new red bow.

As they went down one street they passed two policemen riding great big horses.

"I don't like the policeman on the black horse," said Janine. "He's not smiling like the other one. He looks cross."

“Policemen don’t smile all the time,” said her father. “But, remember, Janine, if you ever need help, ask a policeman. He will know what to do.”

“Isn’t a policeman a stranger?” asked Janine. “Mummy says I must never talk to strangers.”

“Policemen are strangers, that’s true,” said her father, “but they know how to help little girls, and they’re easy to recognise because of their uniform.”

Holding her father's hand, Janine skipped along happily. Soon, they heard the steelbands, and Janine began to dance. Even her father joined in.

But the further they walked, the more crowded the street became, so her father lifted Janine onto his shoulders. She was taller than everyone now.

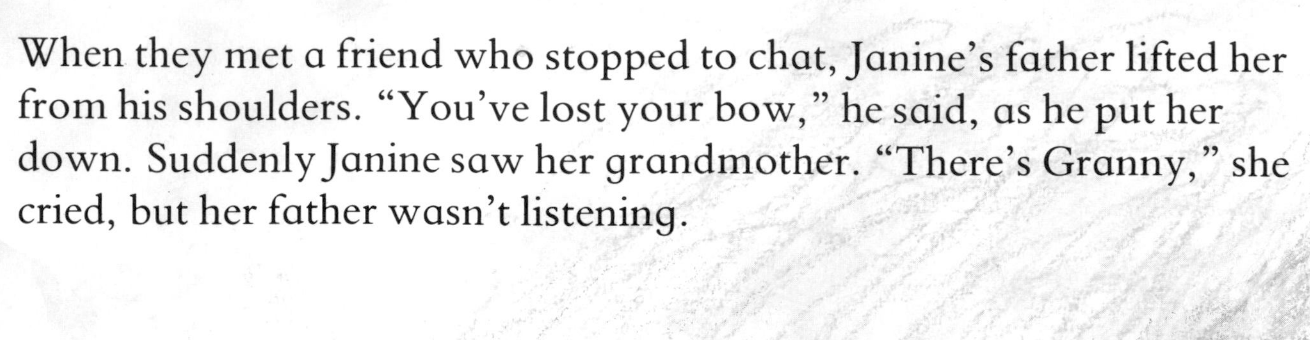

When they met a friend who stopped to chat, Janine's father lifted her from his shoulders. "You've lost your bow," he said, as he put her down. Suddenly Janine saw her grandmother. "There's Granny," she cried, but her father wasn't listening.

Janine thought how pleased he would be to see Granny, so she darted after the lady in the blue jacket.

Suddenly her grandmother disappeared in the crowd. She turned to tell her father, but she couldn't see him either.

Janine was lost. She sat down on the pavement and began to cry.
"What's wrong?" asked a friendly, fat lady. "Are you lost?"
Janine looked up.

“I’m not allowed to speak to strangers,” she mumbled.

“Quite right, too,” said the lady, “but, will you speak to a policeman?”

Janine nodded, remembering what her father had told her.

The fat lady went off, and soon came back with a smiling policeman.

"Hallo, little boy," said the policeman, "are you lost, then?"

"I'm not a boy," Janine answered crossly. "I'm a girl and my name is Janine."

"Sorry," said the
policeman, "I thought
you were a boy because of
your shorts and t-shirt.

Anyway, why don't
you come with me and we
will try to find your parents?"

"Only if you tell me your name," said Janine. "I told you mine."

The policeman bent down. "My name's Peter," he explained, "and I'm going to take you to the Lost Children's Tent."

Janine liked Peter. She told him her address, her telephone number, and how old she was. Then she told him about her mother having to stay at home with the baby.

"You know a lot for a little girl, don't you?" said Peter. "All that will help us find your dad."

The tent was full of children, all crying for their parents.

"You are not going to cry, are you?" asked Peter.

"I might," said Janine. "What if Daddy goes home without me, he doesn't know where I am. And I am hungry."

"We'll soon put that right," said Peter. He gave Janine a drink and some biscuits, and then went off – "to look for your dad," he said.

It seemed a long time before Peter came back, and when he did he was on his own.

"No sign of your dad," he said, "we'll have to phone your mother."
After Peter had told her mother where Janine was, he called her over to the phone. Janine cried when she heard her mother's voice, and her mother was upset too. But then she got cross. "Just wait till you get home," she said. "Running off like that . . ."
"I didn't run off," said Janine, "I just went to meet Granny."

Peter took the phone again, and was just explaining that they would send Janine home in a police car when her father turned up, looking hot and tired.

"Where did you go?" he asked crossly, as Janine hugged him, "I've been looking everywhere for you."

"I saw Granny," Janine explained. "She was looking for us. But she disappeared and I got lost."

"You must never go off on your own," said her father sternly, "even if you think it's safe, never."

"I won't," said Janine, "I'm sorry, Daddy. Mummy's cross and now you are too," and she began to cry again.

"Cheer up," said her father. "I've found you and everything's fine now."

"No it isn't," said Janine. "Mummy's *very* cross. She said 'wait till you get home'."

Daddy gave Janine a hug, then he winked. "Mummy was worried," he said, "that's why she was cross. But when she sees you she'll be so pleased you're safe, she'll give you a big kiss. Just you wait and see."

Janine knew her father was right. Mummy always came round in the end.